My Book of
FAIRY
TALES

W
FRANKLIN WATTS
LONDON·SYDNEY

CONTENTS

Hansel
and
Gretel

Retold by Anne Walter

Illustrated by David Lopez

Once, two children called Hansel
and Gretel lived with their father and
stepmother near the woods.

The family was very poor.
"Take the children to the woods,
there is no food left for them here,"
said the stepmother.

Sadly, the father led his children into
the woods. "Try to find some food here,"
he said. Then he crept away.

"How will we find our way home?"
Gretel asked. Hansel took out his last
crust of bread.

"I will drop these breadcrumbs as we
walk," Hansel said. "We can follow them
back home later."

They walked deep into the woods.

Soon they were tired and hungry.

"Let's go home," said Gretel.

But when Hansel looked behind him,

the breadcrumbs had gone!

"Oh no!" he cried. "We're lost!"

So Hansel and Gretel kept
walking. They walked until
they could walk no more.

Suddenly they saw a house and
ran towards it.

"Look!" cried Gretel. "The roof
is made of gingerbread!"

"And the door is ALL chocolate!"

said Hansel,

munching

greedily.

They ate

and ate

until ...

CREAK! The cottage door opened.

"You poor children," said a little old
lady, smiling. "How hungry you are!
There's plenty more food inside."

So Hansel raced into the cottage and
Gretel followed.

Then, SLAM! The little old lady shut
the door and laughed a wicked laugh.
She was really a witch!

"Now you have eaten my house,
I am going to eat you!" she cried.

Hansel and Gretel were scared.

"But you're both too thin to eat,"
the witch growled, poking them.
"I'll have to fatten you up first."

The witch fed them every day.
She made Gretel work hard and
locked Hansel in a cage so they
could not escape.

The witch could not see very well. She felt Hansel's finger to check how fat he was. When Gretel saw this, she made a plan.

"Hansel, hold out this chicken bone
instead of your finger. It is much
thinner," whispered Gretel.

"Still too thin!" shouted the witch
as she grabbed the chicken bone.

The witch grew tired of waiting.

"I will eat you now!" she cried.

"Get in that oven, girl!"

"But I'm too big!" said Gretel.

"Nonsense," said the witch.

"Even I can fit inside there!"

"How?" asked Gretel, cleverly.

"Silly girl, like this," the witch said.

Gretel rushed to the oven door and
slammed it shut. The witch was
trapped inside.

Then Gretel unlocked the cage and let
Hansel out. They were free!

The witch's house was full of
treasure! Hansel and Gretel filled
their pockets with jewels and went
to find their father.

When they got home, Father was
delighted. Their stepmother had left
and he had been looking for them.
They all lived happily ever after.

The Three Little Pigs

Retold by Anne Walter

Illustrated by Daniel Postgate

Once upon a time, there were

three little pigs.

One day, their mother said, "You're old enough to build your own houses now. But beware of the big bad wolf!"

Soon the three little pigs met a man
carrying straw.

"Please may I have some straw?"
asked the first little pig.

"Yes," replied the man.

The first little pig quickly built a house
of straw.

Next, they met a man carrying sticks.
"Please may I have some sticks?" asked
the second little pig.
"Of course," replied the man.

The second little pig quickly built a
house of sticks.

Then the third little pig met a man carrying bricks. "Please may I have some bricks?" he asked.

"Certainly," replied the man.

The third little pig worked all week long on his house of bricks.

The big bad wolf soon knocked at the

first little pig's door.

"Little pig, little pig, let me in!"

he called.

The first little pig remembered what his mother had told him.

"Not by the hairs on my chinny chin chin!" he replied.

"Then I'll huff and I'll puff and I'll blow your house in!" roared the wolf. He huffed and he puffed and he blew the straw house down.

The first little pig fled to his
brother's house.

The big bad wolf knocked at the
second little pig's door. "Little pig,
little pig, let me in!" he called.

"Not by the hairs on my chinny

chin chin!" replied the second

little pig, shaking.

"Then I'll huff and I'll puff and I'll
blow your house in!" roared the wolf.
He huffed and he puffed and he blew
the stick house down.

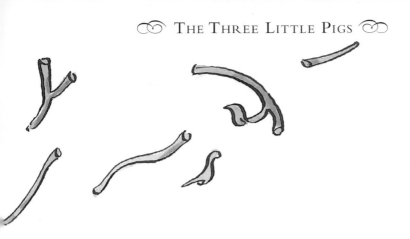

The two little pigs fled to

their brother's house.

The big bad wolf knocked at the third little pig's door. "Little pig, little pig, let me in!" he called.

"Not by the hairs on my chinny chin chin!" came the reply.

"Then I'll huff and I'll puff and I'll blow your house in!" roared the wolf again.

"Just you try it!" called the third little
pig, cheekily.

The wolf huffed and he puffed …

and he huffed and he puffed …

but he could not blow that brick house down.

The wolf was very angry. He decided to climb onto the roof and down the chimney to get his dinner.

Up he climbed ...

in he squeezed ...

and down he

dropped ...

... straight into the third little pig's cooking pot!

PLOP!

The wolf was never seen again!
The three little pigs celebrated
with a big party.

POP!

Little Red Riding Hood

Retold by Anne Walter

Illustrated by Marjorie Dumortier

Long ago, a girl called
Little Red Riding Hood
lived in a village by a wood.

One day, her mother said, "Little Red Riding Hood, your granny is poorly. Please take her this basket to cheer her up.

"But remember – don't talk
to any strangers on the way,"
she added.

Little Red Riding Hood set off straight
away. She had not gone far when she
felt a tap on her shoulder.

It was the big bad wolf!
"What a tasty snack she will
make," he thought.

"Are you lost, little girl?"
asked the wolf, smiling.

"No," said Little Red Riding Hood.

"I'm going to visit my granny.

She lives by the stream."

"Really!" grinned the wolf,

licking his lips.

Little Red Riding Hood picked up the
basket and hurried on her way.

The wolf also rushed to Granny's house.
"Granny lunch with little girl pudding –
delicious!" he thought.

The wolf knocked on Granny's door.

"Come in dear," called Granny.

The wolf let himself in and

swallowed Granny whole!

Then the wolf quickly put on
a nightgown and frilly cap,
and got into Granny's bed.

Soon, Little Red Riding Hood arrived.

"Granny, it's Little Red Riding Hood."

"Come in, dear!" called the wolf in his

squeakiest voice.

When Little Red Riding Hood
went inside, she could hardly
recognise Granny.

"Oh, Granny, you sound terrible!" said
Little Red Riding Hood.

"I have a cold, dear," said the wolf.

"Granny, what big ears you have!"
said Little Red Riding Hood.

"All the better to hear you with,"
replied the wolf.

"Granny, what big eyes you have!"
said Little Red Riding Hood.
"All the better to see you with,"
replied the wolf.

"Granny, what big teeth you have!"
said Little Red Riding Hood.

"All the better to EAT you with!"
roared the wolf and he leapt out of
the bed.

Little Red Riding Hood ran as fast as she could out of Granny's house.

"Help! Help!" she screamed.

The wolf tried to run after her, but he tripped over the nightgown.

Luckily, a woodcutter was nearby.
He grabbed the wolf and made him
cough up Granny.

Then the woodcutter chased the wolf
far away, deep into the wood.

Little Red Riding Hood and Granny
sat down to share the tasty cake from
Mother's basket.

"I promise never to talk to strangers again," said Little Red Riding Hood.

The Emperor's New Clothes

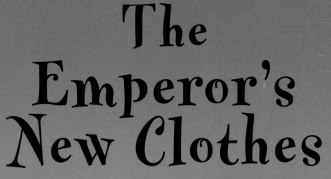

Retold by Barrie Wade

Illustrated by O'Kif

Once there lived a vain emperor

who loved to show off

in new clothes.

One day, two weavers came to his palace. "We can weave you the best robes in the world," said one.

"Our beautiful cloth is so fine that stupid people cannot even see it!" said the other.

"Fantastic," said the emperor. "There is
a procession next week and I want to
wear the grandest robes ever made."

The vain emperor gave the weavers
a bag of gold and a room in the
palace. The cheating weavers
pretended to work.

Everyone wondered what the emperor
would wear for the royal procession.

"The weavers are making a special cloth. It is so fine that stupid people cannot see it!" said the royal maid.

Royal procession Next week

The emperor sent his prime minister
to see the weavers.

"Look at the splendid colours!"
said one weaver.

"Look at the beautiful pattern!"
said the other. The prime minister
could not see anything, but he did
not want to seem stupid.

"What splendid colours! What a beautiful pattern!" he reported to the emperor.

So the emperor sent the weavers
another bag of gold.

Later, the emperor sent his chancellor to
see how the weavers were getting on.

"Look at the lovely colours! Look at the marvellous pattern!" said the cheating weavers.

The chancellor had not seen anything either, but he did not want to admit he was stupid.

"What lovely colours! What a
marvellous pattern!" he reported to the
emperor. The emperor gave the weavers
another bag of gold.

At last the weavers carried the finished cloth to the emperor.

"Look at the marvellous pattern!"
said the chancellor.

"Look at the splendid colours!"
said the prime minister.

The emperor looked, but he could not see anything. However, he did not want to seem stupid.

"How magnificent!" he said.

The procession was the next day.

The cheating weavers pretended to

cut and sew the cloth into robes.

At last they cried: "The emperor's new robes are ready."

The emperor took off his clothes and
the weavers pretended to dress him in
his new robes.

"A perfect fit!" all his ministers cried.
They could not see anything, but
nobody wanted to seem stupid.

The cheating weavers quickly left with
their gold.

The emperor walked in the procession with his ministers. In the streets, the people cheered.

"What a magnificent robe!" they cried. They could not see anything either, but nobody wanted to appear stupid.

Suddenly a child pointed, yelling:

"The emperor has got nothing on!"

"That's right!" the people shouted.

"He's got nothing on!"

Everyone laughed. The vain emperor
blushed and felt very, very stupid.

Snow White

Retold by Maggie Moore

Illustrated by The Pope Twins

Once there was a princess
named Snow White.

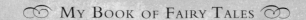
Snow White's stepmother, the queen,
was beautiful but very vain.

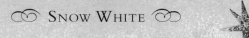

She always asked her magic mirror:

"Mirror, mirror on the wall,

who's the fairest of them all?"

Every time the mirror replied:

"Queen, you are the fairest in

the land."

As Snow White grew older,

she grew more beautiful.

Then one day, when the queen asked her mirror who was the fairest of all, she got a shock.

The mirror told her:

"Snow White is the fairest

in the land."

The queen was furious. She ordered a huntsman to take Snow White into the forest and kill her.

But the kind huntsman felt sorry for Snow White and let her go.

Snow White ran far into the forest and found a little house. Seven dwarfs lived there.

Snow White stayed and looked after the house while the dwarfs worked. They were all very happy.

One day, the queen asked her mirror
again who was the fairest.
"Snow White is the fairest in the land,"
it still replied.

The queen realised that the huntsman
had tricked her. She quickly sent her spies
to find Snow White.

When the queen found out where
Snow White was hiding, she decided
to get rid of Snow White herself.

First, she dressed up as an old woman
and went to the little house to trick
Snow White.

The queen tied ribbons so tightly around Snow White's waist that she could not breathe.

Luckily, the dwarfs arrived just in time to save her.

Next, the queen sold Snow White a
poisoned comb and pushed it into
her hair.

Again, the dwarfs found her
before it was too late.

Finally, the queen tricked
Snow White into eating
a poisoned apple.

But this time the dwarfs were too late.

They put Snow White into a glass

case and looked after her.

The next day, a prince rode by and
saw Snow White in the glass case.
He thought she was the most
beautiful girl he had ever seen.

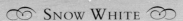

SNOW WHITE

He wanted to take Snow White

to his palace.

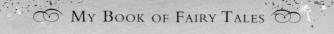

As the prince's men lifted Snow White from the case, the apple fell from her throat. She sat up and saw the prince.

They fell in love at once!

Snow White and the prince invited
the wicked queen to their wedding.
But the queen was so angry that
she ran away and was never
seen again.

Goldilocks
and the
Three Bears

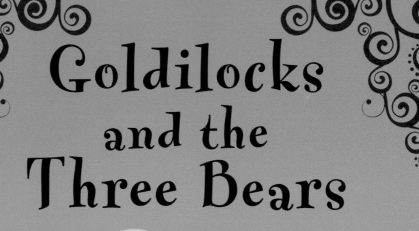

Retold by Anne Walter

Illustrated by Anni Axworthy

Once upon a time, a little girl

called Goldilocks went for

a walk in the woods.

Three bears were also out in the woods.
Their porridge was too hot, so they
had decided to go for a walk while it
cooled down.

Goldilocks found the bears' house in a part of the woods that she had never seen before.

By now, she was very hungry and she could smell something delicious coming from inside the house.

Goldilocks walked in and saw the
three bowls of porridge. First, she
tried the porridge in the biggest bowl.
"Ouch! Too hot!" she cried.

Next, Goldilocks
tried the porridge
in the medium-
sized bowl.
"Yuck! Too cold!"
she said.

Then she tried
the porridge in
the smallest bowl.
"Just right!" she
said, eating it
all up.

After breakfast, Goldilocks wanted
a rest. She sat in the biggest chair.
"Ouch! Too hard!" she cried.

Next, she sat in the medium-sized chair.

"Yuck! Too soft!" she cried.

Then she tried the smallest chair. "Just right!" she said. But as she was getting comfortable ...

CREAK

CRASH!

The chair broke into little pieces.

Goldilocks went upstairs and found
three beds. She lay down on the
biggest bed. "Ouch! Too hard!"
she said.

Next, Goldilocks tried the medium-sized bed. It was so soft that it nearly swallowed her up!

Then she tried the smallest bed.

It felt just right and she fell

fast asleep.

Meanwhile, the three bears were
finishing their walk.
"Shall we see if our porridge has
cooled down?" asked Mummy Bear.

"Yes," Baby Bear replied, "I'm hungry!"
So the three bears hurried back for
their breakfast.

"Who's been eating my porridge?"
roared Daddy Bear.
"Who's been eating my porridge?"
asked Mummy Bear.

"Who's been eating my porridge?"
cried Baby Bear. "They've eaten it
all up!"

"Who's been sitting in my chair?"
roared Daddy Bear.

"Who's been sitting in my chair?"
asked Mummy Bear.

"Who's been sitting in my chair?
They've broken it!" cried Baby Bear.

"Who's been sleeping in my bed?"
roared Daddy Bear.

"Who's been sleeping in my bed?"
asked Mummy Bear.

"Look! Someone's still sleeping
in my bed!" whispered Baby Bear.
"YES!" roared Daddy Bear, loudly.

Grrrrrrr!

Goldilocks woke up immediately.
She jumped out of the window and
ran home as fast as she could.

"What a rude little girl!"

said Daddy Bear.

The Three Billy Goats Gruff

Retold by Wes Magee

Illustrated by Julian Burnett

Long ago, there were three
Billy Goats called Gruff.

One was small, one was medium-sized, and one was big. In spring, the three Billy Goats Gruff felt hungry.

They decided to climb the mountain
to find the sweet grass.

The Billy Goats Gruff came to a rushing river with a wooden bridge. Beneath the bridge lived an ugly troll.

The troll had a lumpy nose and ears like spears. If anyone tried to cross the bridge he would jump out and gobble them up!

"I'll cross the bridge,"
said the small Billy Goat Gruff.
Trippity-trap went his small hooves on
the wooden planks.

"Who's crossing my bridge?" roared the

ugly troll.

"Me," said the small Billy Goat.

"I'm hungry."

"So am I," growled the troll.

"And I'm going to gobble you up!"

"But I'm only small," wailed the little goat. "Wait for my brother, he's bigger than me!"

The troll scratched his lumpy nose.
"Okay," he growled, and the small goat
went *trippity-trap* across the bridge and
ran up the mountain.

"I'll cross the bridge," said the medium-sized Billy Goat Gruff. *Trippity-trippity-trap* went his medium-sized hooves on the wooden planks.

"Who's crossing my bridge?"
roared the ugly troll.

"Me," said the medium-sized Billy
Goat. "I'm hungry."

"So am I," growled the troll. "Very hungry, and I'm going to gobble you up!"

"But I'm only medium-sized," wailed the medium-sized Billy Goat. "Wait for my big brother. He's much bigger than me!"

The troll scratched his lumpy nose.
"Okay," he growled, and the
medium-sized Billy Goat went
trippity-trippity-trap across the bridge.

"I'll cross the bridge," said the big Billy Goat Gruff. *Trippity-trippity-trippity-trap* went his big hooves on the wooden planks.

"Who's crossing my bridge?"
roared the ugly troll.

"Me," said the big Billy Goat.

"I'm hungry."

"So am I," growled the troll.
"Very, very hungry, and I'm going
to gobble you up!" The troll
jumped onto the bridge,
showing his sharp teeth.

The big Billy Goat Gruff lowered his big horns and charged at the ugly troll. He butted him in the middle of his fat tummy. With a cry, the troll went up into the air.

SPLASH! The troll fell into the rushing river and was swept away.

"Now for that sweet grass," said the big Billy Goat Gruff.

He went *trippity-trippity-trippity-trap*
across the bridge and ran up
the mountain.

The three Billy Goats Gruff grew
fat on the sweet grass.

And the ugly troll?

He was never seen again.

Jack and the Beanstalk

Retold by Anne Adeney

Illustrated by Tim Archbold

Long ago, there lived a poor boy

named Jack. He sold milk from

his cow, Milky-white.

One day, Milky-white had no
milk left.

"You must sell her at the market,"
said Mother.

On the way to the market, Jack met an
old man. He told Jack:

"I'll swap these magic beans for your
cow. They will make you rich!"

Jack took the beans and ran home.
"I've swapped Milky-white for some
magic beans!" he said.

"You stupid boy!" shouted Mother,
throwing the beans out of the
window. "Now we will starve."

Jack woke up hungry. Outside his window he saw a huge beanstalk. "The beans were magic!" he cried.

The beanstalk reached high into the sky.

Jack climbed up and up.

At the top of the beanstalk, Jack saw
a huge castle and a giantess. The kind
giantess gave Jack some food.

Suddenly there was a loud crash.

"That's my husband," she said.

"Quick, hide!"

"**Fe fi fo fum**, I smell the blood of an Englishman! Be he alive or be he dead, I'll grind his bones to make my bread!" roared the giant.

"Nonsense! You smell the cow I cooked for breakfast," said his wife.

After breakfast, the giant counted his
gold. Soon he fell asleep.
Jack quietly snatched the gold.

Then Jack raced home. Mother was delighted and they lived richly for weeks.

Soon, Jack climbed up the beanstalk again. "My husband was angry about his gold," said the giantess.

Jack heard the giant coming and hid in the oven.

"**Fe fi fo fum**, I smell ..."

"Fiddlesticks! You smell the sheep I stewed for lunch," said his wife.

After lunch, the giant got out a hen

and ordered:

"Lay, hen, lay!"

The hen laid a golden egg.

Soon the giant was snoring. Jack

grabbed the hen and dashed for

the beanstalk.

"This hen will lay golden eggs for us,
Mother," said Jack. "We will never
starve again."

Later, Jack wondered how the giantess was. He climbed up the beanstalk again.

"You are brave to come back," said the
giantess. "My husband could eat you in
one mouthful! Quick, hide
in here!"

"**Fe fi fo fum** ..." roared the giant.
"Silly giant! The only thing you smell
is the pig I've roasted for supper," said
his wife.

After supper, the giant took out a

golden harp to play a tune.

"Play, harp, play!" he ordered. The

harp played until the giant slept.

Jack seized the harp and ran.

But the harp cried out: "Help!

I am stolen, Master!"

The angry giant woke up and chased
Jack down the beanstalk. Jack hurried
down as fast as he could and yelled:
"Quick, Mother, get me an axe!"

As the giant roared with rage, Jack chopped down the beanstalk.

The giant was never seen again
and everyone lived happily
ever after.

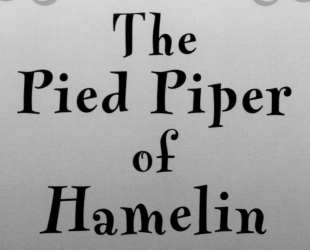

The
Pied Piper
of
Hamelin

Retold by Penny Dolan

Illustrated by Martin Impey

Once there was a rich town
where the people had
plenty of everything.

There were certainly plenty of rats
in the town! They stole food from
the dishes.

They made nests in every
bed and cupboard.

They fought the dogs …

… and chased the cats!

The rats even bit the babies!

"You must get rid of the rats!"

the people told the mayor.

So the mayor put up a poster and

offered a reward to remove the rats.

The people waited and waited.

One day, a tall man appeared.
He was dressed in strange clothes
of different colours.

"I am the Pied Piper and I can get rid
of your rats. But you must pay me a
thousand gold coins," he said.

The mayor whispered something to his deputy. Then he spoke loudly: "Piper, of course we will pay you your reward."

As the Pied Piper stepped into the street,
he began to play a magic tune. All the
rats stopped and listened.

The rats came running after the Pied
Piper. They ran faster and faster.

The Piper stopped at the river, but his music did not. Nor did the rats.

They ran straight into the rushing river,

and that was the end of them!

When the Pied Piper went to ask
for his reward, the mayor laughed.
"You fool! The rats are gone now.
Take these few coins, and get out!"

The Piper was very angry.

"You will be sorry you broke

your promise to me," he said.

The Piper went out into the street.

He lifted his pipe to his lips, and blew.

At once, all the children ran from

the houses.

The children sang and danced, and laughed. They followed the Pied Piper's wonderful tune right out of the town.

Everyone was alarmed.
"Stop him! Pay him!" they
shouted at the mayor.

"He cannot take them far," laughed
the mayor. "Look, the mountain is in
his way."

However, as the Pied Piper reached the mountain, it opened up.

All the children followed the Piper and his music to a beautiful land.

Then the rocks closed. The children and
the Pied Piper were never seen again.
Only one poor child was left outside
the mountain.

Forever afterwards, the people of that
town were sad and silent.

How the mayor wished he had kept his promise!

Cinderella

Retold by Anne Cassidy

Illustrated by Jan McCafferty

Once upon a time there was
a girl called Cinderella.
She was not happy.

Cinderella had two stepsisters.
One was tall and one was small.
They made Cinderella work all
day long.

The stepsisters made Cinderella wear horrible clothes.

And they made her sleep by the fireplace.

One day a letter arrived. "It's from the prince!" said the tall stepsister. "There's a ball at the palace!" said the small stepsister.

Everyone was excited – even Cinderella. The stepsisters told her: "But you can't come!"

After the stepsisters left for the ball,

Cinderella sat by the fireplace.

"It's not fair," she said. "I'd love to go

to the ball!"

Suddenly there was a big flash.

It was a fairy with a wand!

"I'm your fairy godmother," she said.

"Now you can go to the ball!"

The fairy godmother waved her wand.
In another flash, Cinderella had a new
dress and sparkling glass slippers.

Then the fairy godmother

saw a pumpkin ...

four black mice ...

and a rat.

She waved her wand and, in a flash, there were four black horses and a handsome coach driver.

"Here is your coach," she said.

"Now I really can go to the ball!"
said Cinderella.

"Be back before the clock strikes twelve!"
said the fairy godmother.

"Bye bye!" Cinderella said.

"Don't forget to be back by twelve!"
the fairy godmother shouted.

When Cinderella arrived at the ball,
everyone looked at her.

"Who is she?" they wondered.

The stepsisters stared, and the prince
couldn't take his eyes off her.

"Will you dance with me?" the prince asked Cinderella.

The prince and Cinderella danced …

and danced …

and danced all night.

Suddenly Cinderella heard the clock strike twelve. She ran out of the palace. The prince ran after her, but Cinderella was gone.

"Look! She has left a glass slipper
behind!" the prince cried. "Whoever
can fit into the slipper will be my
princess," he promised.

The prince searched every house in the land. Finally, he arrived at Cinderella's house.

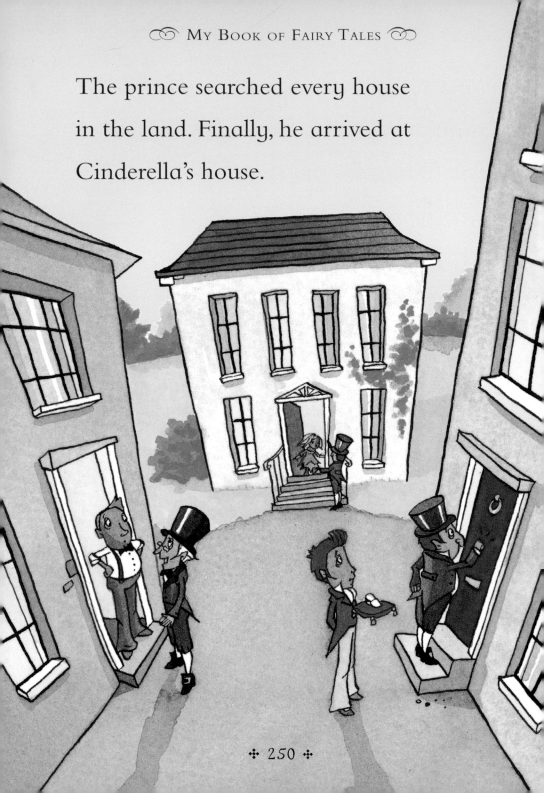

First, the tall sister tried the slipper on.

But it was much too small.

Then the small stepsister tried it on.

But it was much too big.

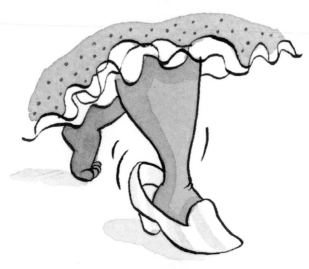

"Now this girl must try it on!"
the prince said.

"But that's just Cinderella!"
laughed the stepsisters.

Cinderella sat down. She tried the glass slipper on. It fitted perfectly.

"Will you be my princess?" asked the prince. Cinderella agreed and they lived happily ever after.

First published in 2014 by
Franklin Watts
338 Euston Road
London NW1 3BH

Franklin Watts Australia
Level 17/207 Kent Street
Sydney NSW 2000

Text Hansel and Gretel, The Three Little Pigs,
Little Red Riding Hood, Goldilocks and the Three Bears
© Franklin Watts 2014, Text The Emperor's New Clothes
© Barrie Wade 2014, Text Snow White © Maggie Moore 2014,
Text The Three Billy Goats Gruff © Wes Magee 2014, Text Jack and
the Beanstalk © Anne Adeney 2014, Text The Pied Piper of Hamelin
© Penny Dolan 2014, Text Cinderella © Anne Cassidy 2014.

The illustrator acknowledgements on pages 4, 26, 54, 80, 108, 132,
156, 184, 206, 230 consititute an extension of this copyright page.

Illustrations © of the individual illustrators credited 2014

A CIP catalogue record for this book is available
from the British Library.

ISBN 978 1 4451 2737 8

Editor: Jackie Hamley
Designer: Chris Fraser
Cover designer: Cathryn Gilbert

Printed in China

Franklin Watts is a division of Hachette Children's Books,
an Hachette UK company.

www.hachette.co.uk